MOG IN THE FOG

for Tom

MOG in the FOG

by Helen Nicoll
and Jan Pieńkowski

PUFFIN BOOKS

ighest mountain in the world

A Sherpa saw them land

Up and up and up and up they climbed

It started to snow

Tsing took them to a cave

The sun
came out.
It was
dazzling

Mog found some footprints

A huge cloud came down

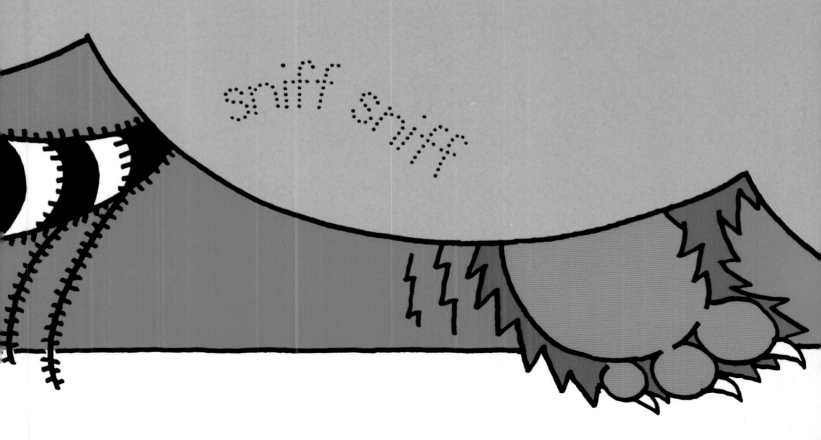

They were lost in the fog

Stay where you are!

I must just find Mog

The fog started to lift

They all ran

and
did
not
stop
until
the
top

Goodbye!